to Eve
D.L.

First published in Great Britain in 2007 by Gullane Children's Books
This paperback edition published in 2008 by

Gullane Children's Books

185 Fleet Street, London, EC4A 2HS
www.gullanebooks.com

1   3   5   7   9   10   8   6   4   2

Text and Illustrations © David Lucas 2007

The right of David Lucas to be identified as the author and illustrator
of this work has been asserted by him in accordance with the
Copyright, Designs and Patents Act, 1988.
A CIP record for this title is available from the British Library.

ISBN: 978-1-86233-726-8

Printed and bound in Malaysia

Something to Do

David Lucas

GULLANE
CHILDREN'S BOOKS

There's nothing to do.

There's nothing to do.

Wake up sleepy bear.

There's nothing to do.

We'll go for a walk . . . .

. . . a long walk.

Still nothing.

A stick!
Now we've got something to do.

Snap.

Look! A line.

Look! Another line.

Look! A ladder.

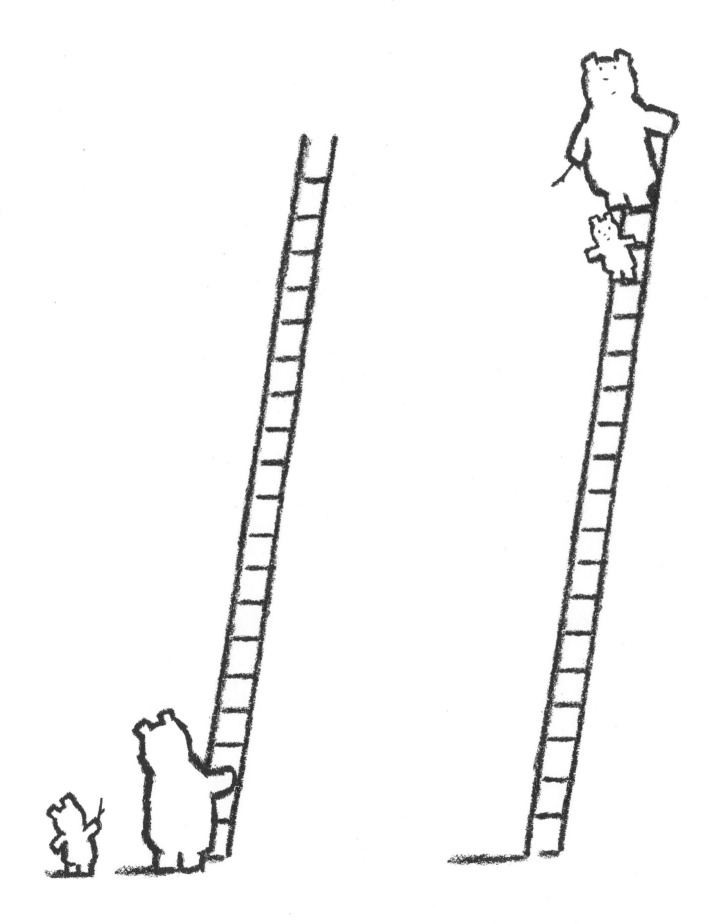

Goodbye ladder!

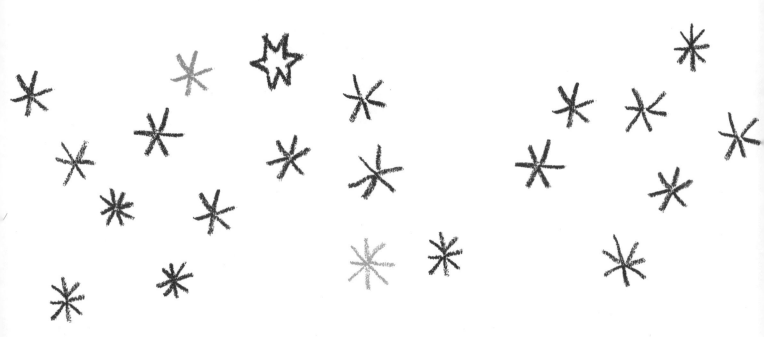

Look! Stars.

Look! A shooting star.

I'm tired.
I'm hungry.

Look! A house.

Knock knock!

Did you find something to do?